# LOVE IS LIKE A REAL RAINBOW: TEXTURE VARIES BUT PURITY STAYS INTACT

By

Dr. HC AGNES JILL TUTO-TURRECHA, M.Ed, RGC

VINEET MANI

**COPYRIGHT © 2021 LOVE IS LIKE A REAL RAINBOW: TEXTURE VARIES BUT PURITY STAYS INTACT**
**By AGNES JILL TUTO-TURRECHA**
**VINEET MANI**



Edited by Marie Ezekiel

Hardbound-978-621-470-139-1
Mobile/Kindle-978-621-470-140-7
Softbound/Paperback-978-621-470-141-4

Published by:
Poetry Planet Book Publishing House
Rosario, Pozorrubio, Pangasinan, Philippines
Contact No.: 09554960044
Email: maritesritumalta@gmail.com

# <u>DEDICATION</u>

*To my daughter, Jillanie Elarine. You are my strength and motivation who encouraged and inspired me to pen down my thoughts in the form of this book. My love for you is overflowing, you are the best creation that God gave to me, you're a blessing not only to our family but also to others as well because of your wit and good character.*

*To my departed parents, I know that it was your dream to see me being successful in my chosen career and here I am now not only I am a registered Guidance Counselor but an emerging author. I can imagine how proud and happy you would be if you were alive. My success is all your success too and this is all for you my beloved parents.*

*To my siblings, relatives and friends who have not only witnessed my journey so far, but who are an integral part of this eventful journey. I may not have materialistic possessions, but I have received His blessings and guidance at every juncture. With His presence by my side, miracles are bound to occur. My every bit is ultimately dedicated to Him*

# <u>TABLE OF CONTENTS</u>


COPYRIGHT...........................................................1

Preface................................................................5

Chapter One-My Childhood Love ...........................7

Chapter Two-They Made Us their Sole Reason to Live ...............................................................22

Chapter Three-They stay as Silent Credible Pillars ...............................................................30

Chapter Four-Life with the Partner- Both Joy & Bumpy Ride .......................................................37

Chapter Five-"My Dream Girl" ...............................44

Chapter Six-Breathe with Flora & Fauna...............51

Chapter Seven-He Has Always Been There..........56

Chapter Eight-They Complete Us..........................61

Chapter Nine-Feel Special to Make Others Feel Special ...............................................................68

About the Author

Profile of Agnes Jill T. Turrecha............................73

A Brief Glimpse- Vineet Mani ...............................75

# **<u>Preface</u>**

We are social beings and what comes natural to us is love. I feel blessed to mention that I had boundless love in my life pouring from all the directions. This pure love which I experienced in various relationships made me cultivate and nurture beautiful traits. Love is fulfilling and gives a sense of direction and beautiful reason to stay alive and happy. It makes you more disciplined, adjusting, caring, loving, affectionate, humble and selfless in many ways.

We shall remember one most important aspect i.e. we cannot expect to get same amount of love that we give in any relationship. It may be disappointing during several occasions, but we shall not cease loving and caring. I have experienced one thing i.e. once we love someone, they may or may not register it, acknowledge it or realize its significance, but they do understand its importance, sooner or later. It is beautifully said that you may have hundreds of reasons to walk out of a relationship, but even one reason may be enough to hold on to it. Why not it be "selfless love"?

My relationship with my husband had a topsy-turvy curve and we had several differences between us. I attempted a lot to make our marriage work, but it did not go well as we used to have during our first year of marriage. But we are together as loving friends for our selfless love for our daughter. I am surrounded by wonderful people- family, friends, colleagues, environment, animal kingdom whose unconditional love and care make my life most incredible, lively and cheerful.

# Chapter One

# My Childhood Love

Not everyone is fortunate to be near the unsoiled and untouched offerings of Mother Nature. Majority of us simply dream to be in the lap of Mother Nature. The islands have their own peculiarity. They are a blend of calmness as the locations are remote and inaccessible, greenery which is so soothing and vast expanse of water all around. Not many are able to visit it during vacations or only a handful get an opportunity to settle down at such a place. I was really lucky as I never had to dream of visiting an island. Agutaya, Palawan, a beautiful unspoiled island is my birthplace and Mother Nature has bestowed all Her rare offerings upon it. The tiny yet splendidly beautiful patch of land boasts of peaceful surroundings, white beaches, various aquatic beings and highly hospitable denizens.

I never experienced hustle-bustle of a city life, long traffic snarls and mindboggling schedules during my childhood days. I was miles away from them. I had pure joy, simple instances of fun and comfort within as part and parcel of my life. I learned the true importance of life and living beings, no matter how tiny. They may be small but are never insignificant. I learned real simplicity and an art to derive immense pleasure from the most ordinary things and situations around me. There were no tall buildings and shopping malls, no public transportation system and materialism was several notches away.

With each day I started growing into a contended and truly happy child and I did not realize when I fell in love with the island. People rightly state that childhood love can never be erased from the memory. Even to this day, I remember ever alley, every grain of sand on the beaches, every instance and every day of my life I spent on and with my 'First Love' as a carefree child.

I was truly lucky to spend my childhood years under the pampering aegis of my most beloved grandparents. They were simple and adorable. They made me learn some great survival skills but most importantly they made me realize the bare fact that there are other living creatures which exist on this Planet and they have equal rights like us. Today, when I read about human-animal conflicts, I cannot comprehend the reason that why humans have to trespass and encroach the territories of those otherwise harmless creatures.

The animals still attack humans as a part of their defense mechanism, but flora avenges in its own way and it is far deadlier. I never experienced it during my early days and I was truly happy with my island, my first love. Though I was just a contended resident, I used to feel that the island is a part and parcel of my life and every fiber of my being belongs to the island. We never expressed it in words, but we stayed in each other's embrace.

I used to feel so secured and joyful and honestly stating, I could never experience it when I came to the city to my parents. I know it for a fact that the island still loves me, remembers me and hasn't changed much. However, I have got changed. Not my love, but my priorities, my responsibilities, my commitments; all have undergone a sea change. But the deeper and covert fact is that I yearn every moment to be back at the island and relive my childhood days ever after.

Well, I was talking about my grandparents who stayed at Concepcion, Palawan, a two-hour ride in pump boat from Agutaya.  In all such regions, the primary livelihood of people even today is fishing. Tourism is gaining grounds, but many are determined not to let the unsoiled beauty and calmness of the islands wither away.

My grandmother was a teacher…a real teacher. She taught me and many like me who were residing on the island rudimentary life skills which helped me survive,

strive and thrive at various fronts. Her style of teaching was gentle, simple yet highly powerful and effective. She never had any elements of favoritism and biasness in the class. She was fair to everyone and each of the student was equally precious to her. I learned the concept of individual attention in a real sense from her. She was thin, fragile, short in height and slightly shy, but her determination was splendid. It seemed to me that she had added potency to her determination derived from the tall waves emanating in the ocean and abundant sunlight all around. She was determined to make me a better contended joyous altruist and she succeeded. She sows those seeds and the harvest was as per her desire. I still feel out of place in the city I reside in as my heart still wanders in the sparsely populated island that never demanded huge rents, seldom inflicted high maintenance and living costs, never added stress in abundance and was unaware of lifestyle diseases. I was a healthy, joyful, carefree soul and the traces are still left within in significant amount.

My grandfather was an adventurous and risk-bearing being, a politician. He was tough but never rough. He was a gentle soul but his way to express love and show concern were different from my grandmother. She brought me closer to learning of all sorts, but my grandfather took me inches closer to the real life and its significance. He used to take me to the beach. My grandmother usually used to accompany me, but he was my permanent companion at the beach. He never left me alone and unattended, but extended adequate opportunities to find my ways independently, explore lesser explored by walking roads less travelled and face difficulties with a brave face.

My grandfather was a sturdy man. Though he had turned old, he was an adventurous man. He always challenged himself every day and that made him overcome his fears.

But what I admired the most about him was his readiness to help anyone and everyone and warmth that stayed intact even when we faced rough patches and adverse situations. Did you ever plan to go to some other big city, grandfather- I used to enquire. I am in love with my island since beginning and I can never part ways with it- he used to state in a simple manner with genuine smile on his face.

My grandparents used to take me to the beach and they trained me how to swim and to catch fish and shells. I used to enter a different fascinating world with crystal clear blue water splashing and dancing waves forming crests and troughs. These swimming lessons and their simple yet deep guidance and companionship made me learn volumes. On one hand, I learned how to collect different kinds of shells for consumption and on other hand, I learned that water never stays calm. The waves rise and may rise beyond imagination and may cause a havoc for which one shall be prepared. Though I was a child, I could relate it to my life as well and when I look back today, I realize how realistic the correlation was. Those lessons to stand tough amidst rough weathers enabled me face various kinds of adversities but I survived and bounced back.

There used to huge paucity of potable water on our island for which we used to travel to different islands to arrange for it.  Significance of every droplet of water. It made me realize the importance of every droplet of water. We seldom wasted water and to us, every drop was precious and priceless. Today when I see people squandering it most irresponsibly, I wish to urge them to stay in such regions where every drop of it counts. When you get something in abundance, you do not mind wasting even a significant portion of it thinking that still a major chunk is left- my grandmother used to teach me such life skills that made me a better being in several respects. My grandfather used to bring practical aspects of what my grandmother used to teach in a simple natural manner.

It made me start thinking and acting in a matured manner and in a responsible fashion, but it never stole mischief and innocence from my childhood. Such thought process made me understand the veritable significance of simplicity and frugal lifestyle. One never need to wear a guise of what s/he is not. No pretensions, no lies and no cunning acts have to be invited to be constant companions once we embrace simplicity- my grandmother's anecdotal accounts on this and other varied topics imbibed simplicity inside me without much efforts and pressure.

Simplicity shall never be confused with absence of joy and fun from life. It is a myth and I am an appropriate example. The way I enjoyed each day at my island, none can never even imagine of it. And imagine who accompanied me always, the Mother Nature. I had a ball of time in Her lap and I never felt need of any materialistic possessions. I had not turned into a sage in any way but was enjoying each moment in the most carefree and splendid manner. It was a matter of envy to many, but who cared.

I enjoyed touching the blue water and watching different creatures and beautiful sceneries around the island. I also experienced picking of "tambalang" or seaweeds and sell it to the store which helped my grandparents to generate income as well. It gave me a sense of being independent and also filled my heart with joy thinking that I could contribute.

I remember visiting the panorama of the beaches, enjoying the mesmerizing beauty scattered all around and my bonding got deepened and strengthened with the amazing aquatic creatures. I was fond of eating and fresh and delicious dishes were available on the island in

abundance. My most favorite seafood was "lato" or grapes in the sea. I also loved tasting the "tilik". It was so delicious that I could continue eating unstoppably. I learned real elements of simple lifestyle and simplicity from my love. They were contended with limited means. They knew how to enjoy life with limited materialistic possessions. I do not know whether they knew that they had the absolute riches bestowed upon them by Mother Nature.

We used to enjoy every morsel like a huge extended family. Most of the residents used to sell fish and tambalang at quite affordable prices. We used to hit the sack very early and wake up when the first rays of the sun used to kiss my childhood love. There used to be load shedding, but we never missed the artificial illumination as we had glittering stars and shining moon.

It is fascinating to share that every single instance of my childhood days, important or trivial is as fresh in my

memory lane as blossoming flowers. I still feel the fragrance and warmth of my childhood love. I seek to reiterate that my life on the island was pure and healthy. It was incomparable and beyond wonderful. Since my childhood, I realized that I derive real happiness in the bounties of Mother Nature. The sense of absolute freedom I breathed and experienced there makes me crave for it every moment.

I could always pour my heart out to flora and fauna, but for humans, I was always an introvert. A bit of lone wolf who could only befriend Nature. Every corner of the island, every leaf on the trees, every rising wave, and every sea creature was and still is a part and parcel of my life. It never changed and seldom will. I used to miss my parents and siblings, but I never sulked and screamed. I could never even think of running away to them. The boundless love of the island and all of its

residents; humans and others very well filled the vacuum. I found solace and real pleasure with them.

They made me to appreciate every detail of stimulus no matter how small it is. And most importantly, a constant immersion into the sea made me remind self that life is so simple, happiness comes in ordinary things and you do not have to wait for the special moments and grand occasions. A simple movement of sea creatures may make you smile and simple view of the crystal-clear blue waters may take you to the lanes of peace and relaxation.

It shall not be surprising to note that a person has great affinity towards sea creatures. It is every bit possible as I fall into that category. I enjoyed being with them, though they didn't know how to express their feelings in human language but they warmly reciprocated my touch and

pure affection for them. Both of us made each other feel important and highly priceless. What a splendid feeling…

Even now when I am under immense pressure, I visit a nearby beach to unwind. I swim for hours and collect shells. The strings of stress and strain seem to get dissolved in the sea water and let me heave a sigh of relief. Not only that, it turns me stronger and tougher to face any rub and difficulty in a composed manner.

I never forget what my childhood love taught me and each time reminds me- 'Magic happens even in seemingly ordinary settings.'

*"Love you forever"*

# Chapter Two

# They Made Us their Sole Reason to Live

They are the initiators. They are ultimate sacrificers. They keep us as their sole and topmost priority. They know the worth of every penny, but keep their concerns aside for our happiness and comforts as it is priceless to them. They derive their happiness and pleasure from our smiles, our achievements and our accomplishments. They are most affected if we encounter slightest of troubles. We may turn thankless and turn our attention away from them, they stay most thankful to Him to blessing them with us and they pray for us every moment. – You guessed it absolutely right. I am talking about our parents. There are volumes and volumes to write

about them and their endless contributions, but there are many things which can purely be experienced and fully enjoyed without expressing much.

We had a huge nuclear family. I have nine siblings and my parents ensured that each gets best upbringing. They took due care of all our needs and basic comforts but luxuries were missing. The best part was that we had boundless love, affection, care and values that kept us most contended and truly joyful. We did not have many materialistic possessions, but with fairness, simplicity, readiness to serve others and pure joy made us most affluent. My father was a simple man and had a real frugal lifestyle. He was a government employee. He worked as a mechanic and his salary was no more than peanuts. The amount was meagre which could not support the needs of the family. My father was determined to meet all the needs of the family for which he used to work during weekends to generate additional income. I do not remember that he ever took a break. He had one thing on his mind i.e. to meet the needs of the family. It was only the needs and comforts of his family which were at the epicenter to him…always. He was veritably thoughtful and kind to all his children in equal proportion. My mother was the best mommy one can ever imagine of or be blessed with. We were ten in number but she ensured that we all receive fair and appropriate attention during all the occasions. It was not only my father who was thoughtful and kind to us, but my mother followed the suit. In fact, she was a huge strength and backbone to the whole family. We used to bicker that who our parents love the most. Today when we siblings sit together we form a consensus and state one thing unanimously- they loved all of us equally.

Sometimes my parents used to tell me that they used to miss me dearly when I stayed with my grandparents on the island. We used to miss you each moment, but we were relaxed

My parents imbibed good values and ensured that we develop strong character. They were strict and can be termed as true disciplinarians. They were soft-hearted within, but they were tough as coconut from outside as they desired us to grow into better beings. Despite all their strictness, we committed mistakes and honestly, we were never spared. We faced consequences and learned a lesson from it.

Due to numerous ongoing struggles and concerns, my parents fell into a sad habit of consuming liquor. They attempted to overcome it, but it acted as a resort to them to wade off the difficulties and troubles at least temporarily. But one thing I wish to proudly wish to declare- They seldom overlooked their responsibilities and duties towards us. They stood by us thick and thin at every stage of life and in every state and situation. They acted as a tower of strength to us. They motivated and encouraged us to overcome all rubs and difficulties, no matter how tall.

Though they are not with us any longer, but I feel their presence around me each moment. They guided me in my professional life, helped me in my personal life and took best care of my daughter when she was little. I could not imagine even me

taking such care of Cris, my lovely daughter. Even after I got married and then got separated from my husband, they stood by me and loved me, cared for me and supported me more than previous times.

I clearly remember every moment I spent under their shade. Each moment with them was beautiful and special. We faced many terrible and miserable situations, but we sailed through as we stood together. I proudly state that my parents are my strength. Though they are not with me in this world, but they are constantly around and take best care of me from another world.

They are always in my heart and act as my torchbearers at every juncture. Whenever I am under distress, I remember them in my heart. I derive inspiration, courage and right direction and feel safe, secured and protected in their permanent

embrace.

*Love you tatay & nanay… till my last breath!*

# Chapter Three

## They stay as Silent Credible Pillars

I remember that we used to fight with each other. Sometimes the issues used to be so trivial that our parents used to get irritated and scold us all to maintain peace and harmony at home. But the kind of fun we used to have was unbelievable. Yes, I am talking of my siblings; most credible and ever-standing pillars of my life. We grew up together and there are numerous instances which indicate togetherness, deep bonding and boundless affection for each other. We fought tooth and nail on many occasions but stood as a single strong unit to fight off various troubles, rubs and difficulties that attempted to haunt us.

I clearly remember that when we lost our mother first and then father, we all lamented, sobbed and felt shattered as one. We cuddled each other. We wept profusely in each other's arms. We consoled each other. There have been many such instances when we came together and shared moments of happiness, joy, sorrow and grief.

Though ours was a nuclear family, but we were ten of us which was like a small brigade. We never felt need of anyone else in our lives. There used to be hustle-bustle at our home and wherever we used to go. As children, we used to go anywhere and everywhere together. We shared all our secrets with each other. Of course, sometimes some brother or sister used to be closer and on other occasions some others. But the bottom line was that we loved each other most dearly and stood for each other thick and thin.

I clearly remember that when my parents used to be in an inebriated condition, elder siblings used to take best care of younger ones. We used to conceal mistakes of each other from our parents to avoid their wrath. Our parents used to feel very proud of the fact that we used stay as a cohesive force, though there used to be times when we strayed or attempt to stray, but used to come back.

I used to feel so strengthened and fearless because of presence of my siblings. It was not only their presence, but their love, care and concern that made me feel strong. I had relationships and my heart was broken as well. They were the ones who let me cry on their shoulders and listened to me for hours so that I vent out all my emotions, frustration and anger. They acted as advisers, counsellors, bodyguards, best buddies and so on. They assumed different roles at different times and one thing remained unchanged: they were always there; undeterred and unfluttered.

We were inseparable in the beginning, but as we were growing up, our paths got different and we went into different directions. We made our choices, some good some grave. We chose our field of specialization and area of working. We made new bunch of friends, got into relationships, started travelling, got married, got kids and started living separately. It is the cycle which every family undergoes. But we were away only in terms of physical distances or due to our busy schedules and commitments, but one call and everyone used to huddle together leaving everything aside, no matter how significant.

We all are different personalities with different temperaments. We are different and so are our thoughts, our experiences, our exposure and our perspectives. Difference of opinions always cropped up amongst us on many occasions, but we stayed inseparable through hearts. We might not be able to catch up with each other very often, but our prayers, support, blessings and care is always there for each other.

We do miss each other's presence dearly during each moment, but there is an assurance that we have each other's back whenever and wherever required.

My siblings not only enabled me to endure immense pain due to my personal struggles, but they also empowered me, made me feel confident to take steps forward and supported in every respect to start my food business. There came many ups and downs at various fronts. The boat of my life almost capsized on many occasions, but my siblings stayed with me holding the oars tightly and firmly.

At any hour of the day or night, if I just call them or drop a message, I find them standing beside me and my daughter and ever-willing to do everything for our wellbeing. Be it financial, mental, moral; their support was boundless. And I reciprocate the same standing by them as it shall be and must be mutual.

We all are trying to instill the same sense of unity, belongingness, care and affection in our next generation as well as the support of siblings is unparallel and may help us overcome any and every adverse situation.

**'Thanks for being with me and mine. We will stay unchanged for each other…ever'**

# Chapter Four

# Life with the Partner- Both Joy & Bumpy Ride

When you are single or dating casually, you are a carefree bird. Even if you are serious in a relationship, you still have chances to wriggle out of it if things go haywire. But marriage is an institution which changes everything. You are bound to make adjustments, fulfill obligations and commitments, curtail your desires and freedom, sacrifice a lot and sometimes beyond and find your happiness in happiness of your partner. Well, it is applicable for both the partners. Until they carry it out well, honestly and sincerely, the marriages work fine and they ultimately turn into long lasting ones.

When I got married with the man of my choice, I was fully prepared and all set to make our married life most beautiful and ever-lasting. It must be exemplary- I used

to remind myself of it every day. The intention of my husband was completely in sync with mine. It all started on a wonderful note. We used to have wonderful moments, loads of fun, great deal of travelling holding hands, teasing each other, cracking jokes, giggling and laughing together, eating, drinking together and watching movies.

Our married life was great in every respect and with passage of time we were blessed with a beautiful angel. She brought freshness, new vitality and excitement in our lives. Our responsibilities got increased manifold, but our love stayed intact. But this is the point where I went wrong. My husband loved our daughter a lot, but he started getting digressed from our family duties slowly and gradually. I could not realize it in the evening and even he was unaware of such misroute.

I made him realize that he is going in the wrong direction and he too realized it. But what became the bone of

contention between us was that I had to remind him of it time and again and the reminders became more frequent. In the beginning, we used to have normal discussion in a calm and composed manner but with increase in frequency, the reminders turned into ugly fights. The allegations and counter allegations, arguments and counter arguments turned it hideous beyond control.

It was not that we never spoke to each other about resolving the differences. We had discussions for hours, we were highly concerned about our daughter and impact of our series of bickering on her, we wept in each other's' arms for hours and made resolutions and promises to mend ways. I decided to be calmer, act more sensibly and responsibly even if I feel miserable from within. I wanted things to be back to normal and so was his objective, but we could not bridge the rift despite our

sincere and repeated attempts. It kept widening and we stayed as mute poor spectators.

I wanted him to come forward to support my food business, but he had decided not to be involved in it. He had his own reasons, but during that time he was thinking only about himself and not us. I was vying for his support, confidence, love, care and affection, but he could not extend it even if he wanted to. One fine day, we decided to get separated. Staying in each other's presence was becoming toxic.

I stayed in our house and started pulling myself together. There were hiccups and losses in my food business but he never cared to find out how pathetic the situation was. He stayed indifferent and slowly from 'everything' we turned into 'non-entities' to each other. I never ever stopped him from meeting our daughter. In fact, he used to pick her up on Saturdays and drop her off during Sunday evening. I wanted my daughter to have love and

care of her father as well and shall never be devoid of it. I always gave due importance to the presence and care of both the parents as what I am today is only because of my most wonderful parents.

But situations change. They worsen and then they turn brighter and positive as well. Gradually, he had a change of heart. We are still separated but we have become thick friends now. We care for each other and still love each other deep down. We do talk of our old memorable moments and try to relive them. We are giving more and more opportunities to each other to come closer and to have the bond stronger and deeper. At one point in time, he never used to pay any heed to my presence even when we were breathing under the same roof, today he takes care of every small thing my daughter and I require. He fulfills our requirements and desires without we even mentioning it.

Things are looking up and they will turn better and brighter is our prayer.

**'We all make mistakes and we must forgive our loved ones to start afresh, especially our life partner.**

# Chapter Five

# "My Dream Girl"

Parenthood is such a splendid feeling which transforms the life completely. It brings a new sense of responsibility, excitement, care and concerns of the next level. A carefree couple turns into parents who are ready to do anything and everything for their child. We also got the most special gift in our lives in the form of my daughter, Jillanie Elarine. I fondly call her Cris. She is a source of my strength and I consider her as bright light in my life. Her presence scatters and dissipates clouds of darkness of every magnitude. No matter how worried I am, her winsome smile leaves me fully relaxed.

She is a true blessing and an inspiration to me. With each passing day, she exhibits great level of innate talents and skills she is acquiring and those acquired, she is mastering them. Jillaine is a highly disciplined

being and has set of high values she follows religiously. We share several relationships with each other. Sometimes we are playmates, on other occasions we are best pals. Some other times we are sisters and we are fashion stylists as well. I shall not forget to mention that we enjoy a wonderful relationship of mentor and disciple as well. She is so chirpy and carefree that dullness, boredom and negativity stay at bay.

Sometimes, I feel very low and lonely as well. She walks up to me and does not utter a word. She looks into my eyes and understands a lot without me expressing anything at all. She cuddles me tightly, kisses me and whispers into my ear- I am with you and will be there forever. Tears of joy well up in my eyes and when I look at her sparkling eyes, there are tears of assurance in hers.

I have always kept Cris away from luxuries but always fulfilled her needs and arranged for basic comforts. I am

a strict parent, but honestly stating, she is a mature, responsible and sensible child who has never let me increase the level of strictness at any point in time. She is my blue-eyed girl and being the only child, I do pamper her. But my lovely pretty daughter has never taken undue advantage of it. We both extend complete support to each other. It is not only I who give her all my attention to her, but she also takes care of every small thing of mine. Keeping an eye on my needs and comforts is her topmost priority and she makes me feel so special all the times.

She is great at academics and also does well at co-scholastic front. She is a consistent performer and is awarded with honors since preschool. She exhibits humility, kindness and respect for everyone. She does not detest her father at all, in fact she loves him, but she loves me the most. She has a magnetic personality which draws everyone's attention towards her but she

has an ability to stay level-headed. She has been a driving force who has brought greater level of sensibility and responsibility in her father.

Cris calls spade a spade but in a polite manner. She confronts me as well if I say or do something wrong but ensure that she never jumps off limits and always remember that I am her mother and much elder to her. She pinpoints towards the points she finds wrong, but she expresses her opinion in a highly respectful and dignified manner so that none shall feel offended and yet she is able to put across her point(s).

There have been numerous moments and phrases that she uses that make me feel so sure and confident that no matter what, she will never desert me. The situations may get worst, but she will stick around and will hold me and herself together. She acted as a great support during the pandemic. She followed all the precautionary measures religiously and compelled me to do so. She allowed no lackadaisical attitude on her part or mine and that was one of the primary reasons how we survived unscathed and unaffected.

One day while we were watching television, she embraced me and said in her soft tone- 'Mama, please don't get old so quickly. I am still a little kid and I want to take best care of you when I grow up. Give me some time.' Her innocence and truthfulness melted my heart forever. Our bonding is getting more and more deepened with each passing day. She never lets me be alone as she knows what I am going through at professional and personal fronts. She holds my hands and tells me that everything is bound to be fine.

She is friends to every friend of mine. She is deeply attached to all her aunts, uncles and cousins. She takes great care of everyone in the immediate and extended family. Her wonderful and heartwarming personality brings a sense of pride in my heart and my face glimmers because of her. As a child, she too wants a lot more, but she knows my limitations. She expresses her gratefulness during all the times for what I do for her. You are The Best Mommy- she keeps telling me.

She is so attached to me that she could not bear my absence. Whenever I am at work, she keeps calling me enquiring when I will be back and urges me to be back soon. She makes me feel valued and has brought meaning and a reason for me to live, smile, thrive and strive forever.

**"I wish to admit that you are my spark and I love you most dearly.**

**Love you forever, my priceless treasure."**

# Chapter Six

# I Breathe with Flora & Fauna

I enjoy great affinity with plants and animals since my childhood. The primary reason was spending considerable time during my childhood on the island where aquatic creatures and tall trees were my constant companions. Over a period of time, I got inclined towards and embraced gardening as a hobby. I love talking to plants while I am in my small garden. I take care of them as my own children and they silently reciprocate. As soon as I step inside my garden, the freshness and fragrance take away all my stress and I feel relaxed. It is a mental spa to me and I love staying in their evergreen company for hours together. It is a new silent serene exuberant world devoid of all malpractices and I just love being there.

In the wake of pandemic, when none could step out of the house, they acted as the constant companions. I share all my problems with them and it seems that they not only listen, acknowledge but do show direction by opening our minds through their freshness, innocence and selflessness. I love to stay with them and simply lose track of time in their incredible company.

I keep reminding myself that their protection is quintessential for our survival and I remind it to every soul I am acquainted with. Their protection and preservation of flora is required to protect our environment, our Planet and our entire race.

As far as animal kingdom is concerned, I have special place in my heart for cats, dogs and birds. I used to have a small fish pond in our yard as Cris was really fond of spending time watching them having fun and frolic. Dogs are considered to be most loyal, trustworthy best friends of humans. I was really fortunate to have three pet dogs

years ago and their names were Ela, Hans and Pongchao. They were truly adorable. They were innocent but they were equally mischievous and funny. Our home used to have hustle-bustle during all the times. There was a strong sense of safety and security and no loneliness within the sight.

My tailed friends used to sense my mood and if I am despondent and feeling low, they would lick my feet, wag their tails, bark happily to make me feel chirpy again. I used to get normal in no time in their incredible company. When I used to be angry or used to scold them, they would hide under the sofas, chairs or beds and used to wait for me to be fine and then use to come out of their hidings.

My daughter, Cris, loved them so much and always caressed them gently. She used to move her hands through their thick soft furs. They seldom left her alone and she had best and most obedient playmates. But moments of joy do not reside in life forever. We were also struck by gloominess when the trio passed away one after another within a short span of time. We had such vacuum in our lives that we were unable to accept it. They left us lonely and sad. We wanted to have new set of friends, but could not muster courage as their presence makes life bright and light, but their demise leaves you shattered and in a state of despair.

However with passage of time, we brought new set of friends in our lives. We are so used to them that we cannot stay without them at all. Now we have Coco and Zooey who are from dog clan and a cat named Jan Lee. They are equally wonderful. However, I still hear the older ones playing, jostling and staying involved in some scrimmages. Sometimes, I call out their names as well to serve their meal but when I turn around, they are not there, but we have most beautiful memories of theirs and gathering amazing memories with the current ones.

**'You were and are great pals and you will always be in our hearts'**

# Chapter Seven

# He Has Always Been There

It is true in everyone's case and I proudly declare that He is my only savior at every turn of my life. Since my childhood, I used to wonder who created this world. I used to look all around in amazement. The more I explored the more I discovered the more I got assured that He exists everywhere and I felt more and more relaxed that He is always there to guide, protect, direct, love and care. We were ten of us and I mentioned in a previous Chapter that my father's income was meagre and both my parents had a bad habit of consuming liquor. But they had absolute faith in Him. We not only used to go to Church every week, but we followed all religious practices which made us inclined towards philanthropy. Complete faith in Him made us stay pious,

pure, transparent and respectful in our thoughts, words and action.

There were several occasions when we lost all our hopes, but never let hopes in Him get dashed. From nowhere, we received help and we were able to overcome most adverse situations. Whenever we use to face any adversity, we as a family used to sit together, close our eyes and used to pray to Him. I was an introvert and used to speak very less. But I got an inspiration directly from Him in some unknown way that I shall exhibit expect to everyone and show reverence to all my elders. I was guided to shower boundless love and affection on the younger ones.

My humility, humbleness and respect for everyone are biggest gifts of His to my life. I underwent struggles galore and had impediments at every step and stage, but

none of it could extinguish my flickering ray of hope. I never lost touch from my sense of responsibility and duty and sensibility to carry them out most efficiently and effectively. I am considered as a hardworking, dedicated, focused and efficient team member at the workplace and I give entire credit to Him as He has been my permanent Guide.

There were complexities in life and I was never sure how are they going to get fixed, but He ensured that clouds of confusion, uncertainties, gloominess evaporate and what stayed on was clarity, peace and light. And it continues… I have witnessed his miracles in my life. All the doors were tightly closed and I could not find a way, but He carved out the path for me to come out unscathed and unaffected.

I lost my parents, went bankrupt, got separated from my husband, and series of big and trivial problems kept haunting me, but He never deserted me. My faith and commitment to God are unparallel. The problems still exist but He has given me immense strength to recover and cope up.

**"Be my light and never let me go out of
Your sight"**

# **Chapter Eight**

# **They Complete Us**

We cannot choose our parents, our siblings, our other family members and relatives, but choosing friends is our choice and purely lies in our hands. I must admit that I have been truly fortunate not to have fair weather friends. I always had friends who stood by my side in every adversity. We may not be in touch with each other very often, but I am assured about one thing i.e. whenever I need them, they will be there. They have proven it numerous times. I looked up to them for help, guidance, assistance, support, understanding, cooperation, love, care and concern and I received it all in abundance and always.

They have taught me a lot and still continue to do so. I spend great deal of time with them when time permits

and it is most enjoyable and comfortable. Over a period of time, I have learned that

Friendship has no written rules and guidelines but only trust and commitment needed to make the relationship work. Friendship is not dependent on age, gender, color of the skin, beauty, nationality or ethnicity. Purity in hearts, being natural always, no pretension and selfless inclination lays down foundation of an ever-lasting friendship. I feel most comfortable to share our fears, worries, challenges, difficulties that we encounter in our lives.

During my High school, I had a few selected friends namely Dece Joy Cepe Cabrera and Leny Pines. They were my best buddies and we share the same bond, in fact, it has grown deeper and stronger. Whenever we meet each other, we remember our good old carefree days and burst into peals of laughter. We happily recall

every moment of joy, fun, frolic, togetherness and also of our bickering. We knew each other's every secret and we still keep it under the wraps. We had a pact never to reveal what is closest to our hearts and what we wish to keep hidden ever and we seldom break it. We knew almost everything about each other and we make it a point to keep each other updated of what is going on in our lives. Whenever we are together, the time simply flies by. We have so much to recall and so much to update to each other. And the best part is that it goes on and on and time always seems to be a constraint as we wish to stay together forever.

During my college days, I got one real genuine friend, Ma Melinda. We used to share all kinds of good moments and bad experiences and her contribution in my life has been significant. We still meet each other, in fact, create

opportunities to meet each other as we simply love each other's company.

I met Adam Gregory who is from the US , he is a great supporter of my undertakings especially to some of my humanitarian involvement. He has a good heart in helping the less fortunate in my community.

Claus Sorensen who hails from Denmark is my friend for almost 4 years, he has a beautiful family with a kind hearted wife , Quennie and a son Carl. He and his family treated me and my daughter as members of their own family. They deeply cared and show concerns for both of us. He also supports my outreach activities in the community.

John is also a great friend from the Philippines, his wisdom about life gave inspiration to me to be resilient and to keep going.

All of my friends exuberate optimism, humility and kindness. They extended unbarred support in some of

my outreach initiatives for the community. They believe in giving and serving and made me understand real meaning and significance of selfless service.

My friend from India, Vineet, who is Co-Author of this book and my first book as well has been a true mentor and selfless advisor to me. He turned my dream of authoring books into a magnificent reality without expecting anything in return. I find his presence highly comforting and fills me with a sense of being strong. He is totally reliable, credible and sincere. Though he hopscotches due to his passion for travelling, he ensures that we stay connected. His promptness is unparallel and his affection towards me and Cris bring tears into my eyes.

He is a wizard when it comes to words and expressions, but he is so level-headed and ever-willing to guide and

support everyone which is indisputably exemplary. His incredible ideas and amazing skillset deserve appreciation and adulation galore. My heart and soul always thank him to be by my side and enabling me to discover my true self and innate potential.

**" *True genuine friends of my life*"**

# Chapter Nine

# Feel Special to Make Others Feel Special

We all take birth and try to do what best we can for ourselves and take best care of our loved ones. It is a wonderful feeling, but what brings immense joy to the heart and the soul is when we walk an extra mile for beings who may not do anything for us in return, but their smiles, relief, blessings and prayers are priceless. They look up to able-bodied people who are better off than them in any respect and we must do what best we can and to the greatest extent possible. My parents taught us to serve anyone and everyone, be it humans, flora and fauna. We used to do our tiny bit for those in need and it got cultivated into a real passion.

I have been so fortunate to be a part of some selected philanthropic entities that operate domestically and internationally. These organizations empowered me and nurtured my human skills and sense of empathy and selfless service. Some of the organizations I am associated with are Global Academy of Human Excellence (GAHE) founded by H.R.H Prof. Jovylyn S. Espalabra. I hold the post of a Provincial Coordinator. I was a Country Coordinator with Impact Youth Sustainability based in Congo Republic which was founded by Nyembo S. Jay and I was chosen as Regional Coordinator by Asia Pacific Society of Volunteers (APSVI).

I feel delighted that my siblings are fully and actively involved with me in a range of outreach activities and community services. Our focus areas are specifically in San Remigio,and Badiang, San Jose, Antique. We are

fully committed, actively involved and absolutely dedicated to serve the lesser-privileged ones, no matter how little is the contribution. My heart stays filled with immense joy, highest level of satisfaction, selflessness, empathy and humility.

It is the most important part of my life and I am determined to continue this divine drive forever.

**"Make the lesser fortunate souls special and enjoy the most splendid feeling yourself."**

# **About the Author**

## <u>Profile of Agnes Jill T. Turrecha</u>

Agnes was born on the beautiful unsoiled island of Agutaya, Palawan. She spent some part of her childhood on that island with her grandparents and members of extended family before moving to the Province of Antique to her parents and has some wonderful memories of it. She graduated as Class Valedictorian in Elementary and 2$^{nd}$ honor under National Secondary Curriculum in High School. Further she completed her graduation in the field of Psychology from the University of Philippines and did her Masters degree in Guidance & Counselling from West Visayas State University. With her tireless efforts, dedication

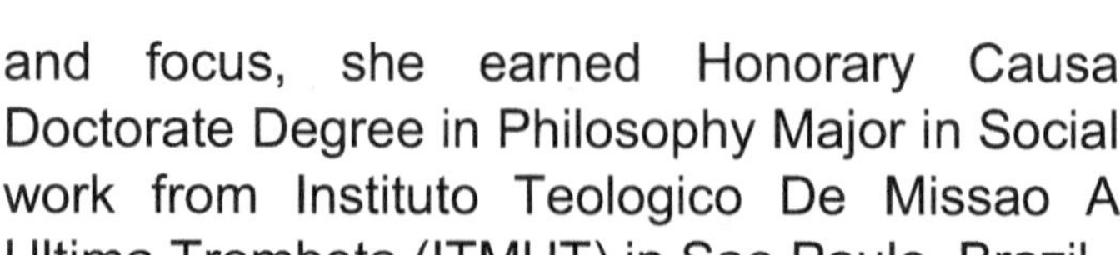

and focus, she earned Honorary Causa Doctorate Degree in Philosophy Major in Social work from Instituto Teologico De Missao A Ultima Trombeta (ITMUT) in Sao Paulo, Brazil.

She has worked in several capacities in some reputed organizations in the region. Agnes is a die-hard entrepreneur and understands the nuts and bolts of business. Despite she faced setback and several hiccups in her food business, she is trying to revive it and bring it back on track. In fact, she has grand plans of diversifying in other fields as well.

Though she is a thorough professional and an emerging businesswoman, she loves to practice and hone her counseling skills and expertise. She is currently working as a Registered Guidance Counselor in a Public High School in the Province of Antique where she resides with her daughter and siblings.

When Agnes is not working on her new books in pipeline along with his Co-author, Vineet, and not working on business revival plans; she loves spending her time doing gardening, cooking and volunteering. She has a soft corner for lesser-privileged people and the society on the whole and she volunteers for some genuine organizations whenever she finds time, in fact, she takes out time for such causes.

# **<u>A Brief Glimpse- Vineet Mani</u>**

A strategist due to qualification, experience and exposure in the field of management, but a dreamer, explorer and expresser out of utmost passion. After working for some highly progressive and organic organizations, he started his own venture named ToHeartsThroughWords, an entity responsible for curating communication strategies and developing content for some selected entities operating in different sectors viz. Education,

FMCG, NGOs, Mining, Travel, Fashion Designing, Image Consulting, Food and others. He loves to express his thoughts and notions in words while on the move. He has emerged as a traveller writer of sorts as well and has visible presence on Google Maps as a Local Guide, TripAdvisor and LinkedIn. Some of his observation papers have been published in some journals. The recent one was picked up by Jamia Milia Islamia University, a Central University of India for the International Conference on Rural Tourism. He firmly believes in working towards sustainable practices and work on ground in this direction individually and with some entities as well. Vineet loves interacting with young minds and visit schools, colleges and varsities to conduct sessions ranging from sessions on email etiquette, motivation, verbal ability, quizzing, group discussions, interview skills and others. When he is not working, Vineet loves to read, do gardening, cook, stalk Royal Bengal Tigers on foot, meander in dense woods and sing.

www.ingramcontent.com/pod-product-compliance
Lightning Source LLC
LaVergne TN
LVHW010249200726
843506LV00014B/3168